the day the goose got loose

by REEVE LINDBERGH
pictures by STEVEN KELLOGG

Dial Books for Young Readers　New York

Published by Dial Books for Young Readers
A Division of Penguin Books USA Inc.
375 Hudson Street, New York, New York 10014

Printed in the U.S.A.
Design by Jane Byers Bierhorst
First Edition
E
1 3 5 7 9 10 8 6 4 2

Library of Congress Cataloging in Publication Data

Lindbergh, Reeve.
The day the goose got loose
by Reeve Lindbergh; pictures by Steven Kellogg.
p. cm.
Summary: The day the goose gets loose, havoc reigns
at the farm as all the animals react.
ISBN 0-8037-0408-9 ISBN 0-8037-0409-7 (lib. bdg.)
[1. Domestic animals—Fiction. 2. Stories in rhyme.]
I. Kellogg, Steven, ill. II. Title.
PZ8.3.L6148Day 1990 [E]—dc19
87-28959 CIP AC

*The full-color artwork was prepared using ink and pencil line
and watercolor washes. It was then color-separated and
reproduced as red, blue, yellow, and black halftones.*

For Eli and Sam and the Lone Gander
R.L.

Love to Amy the Great
S.K.

When the goose got loose
She caused a riot.

Nobody ever thought she'd try it!
There wasn't any more peace and quiet.
The day the goose got loose.

When the goose got loose
The hens were mad.

The goose ate all the grain they had!

The rooster sulked and the chicks were sad.

The day the goose got loose.

When the goose got loose
The sheep were scared.

They huddled together and shivered and stared.

They would have come into the house if they dared!

The day the goose got loose.

When the goose got loose
The ram went wild.

He butted the Bixbys' younger child!

Her dress got messed and her hair un-styled.

The day the goose got loose.

When the goose got loose
The horses were glad.
They kicked up their heels and ran like mad!

The colt was silly.

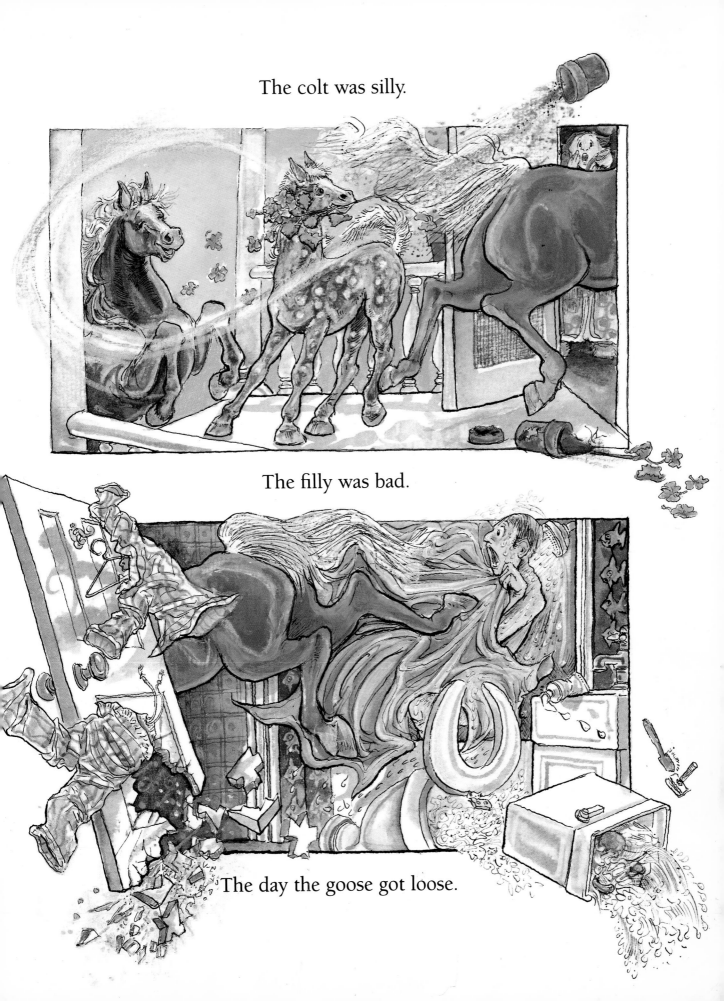

The filly was bad.

The day the goose got loose.

When the goose got loose
The cows were tense.
The goose provoked a bull named Spence.

He charged right through the pasture fence!

The day the goose got loose.

When the goose got loose
Our herd was gone.
They galloped to the courthouse lawn.

The sergeants brought them back at dawn.

The day the goose got loose.

When the goose got loose
My dad was annoyed.

He said this wasn't a day he enjoyed.
His morning routine was completely destroyed.

The day the goose got loose.

When the goose got loose
My mom was upset.
She said the goose was a personal pet.

She walked all around with a butterfly net.

The day the goose got loose.

When the goose got loose
My brother knew why.
He heard the wild geese flying high.

They stood in the meadow and waved good-bye.

The day the goose got loose.

When the goose got loose
My grandmother said,
Quite late in the evening, just before bed,

"I wonder what thoughts went through her head?"

The day the goose got loose.

When the goose got loose

I dreamed a dream

Of a flock of geese in a silver stream,

Some tame and some wild, in a fine-feathered team.

The day the goose got loose.